Cora Harrison was a primary school teacher for
twenty-five-years. Then she moved to a small farm
in Kilfenora, Co. Clare. There is an Iron Age fort at
the farm. There are also a lot of forests around the
farm and Cora loves going for walks there with
her own dog Wolf.

Other books by Cora Harrison

Wolf in the Midnight Forest

The Drumshee Timeline Series
Book 1: *Nuala and her Secret Wolf*
Book 2: *The Secret of the Seven Crosses*
Book 3: *The Secret of Drumshee Castle*
Book 4: *The Secret of 1798*
Book 5: *Famine Secret at Drumshee*
Book 6: *Titanic Voyage from Drumshee*
Book 7: *millennium@drumshee*
Book 8: *The Drumshee Rebels*
Book 9: *The Viking at Drumshee*
Book 10: *Murder at Drumshee*
Book 11: *World War II – Rescue at Drumshee*
Book 12: *Dark Days at Drumshee*
Book 13: *Secret Spy from Drumshee*

For
my grandson, Shane Mason

WOLF
AND THE
FROZEN
MIST

CORA HARRISON

WOLFHOUND PRESS

First published in 2003 by
Wolfhound Press
An Imprint of Merlin Publishing
16 Upper Pembroke Street,
Dublin 2, Ireland
Tel: +353 1 676 4373
Fax: +353 1 676 4368
publishing@merlin.ie
www.merlin-publishing.com

Text Copyright © 2003 Cora Harrison
Design and Layout © 2003 Merlin Publishing

A CIP catalogue record for this book is available
from the British Library.

ISBN 0–86327–920–1

10 9 8 7 6 5 4 3 2 1

Cover Illustration and Design by Graham Thew Design
Internal Illustrations by Helen Smith, Allied Artists
Typeset by Carrigboy Typesetting Services
Printed and bound in Denmark
by Nørhaven Paperback A/S

In the Midnight Forest

The trees of the Midnight Forest were huge. In the white light of the moon, their spiky branches looked like witch's hair. The path beneath the trees was silver-grey. Dark shadows passed in front of them.

Mark and Wolf were on the path leading into the forest. They had almost reached Pamela Pine-Marten's nest.

There was an evil smell. Mark put his hand on Wolf's neck. From time to time, he looked nervously over his shoulder. Some strange shape seemed to be moving behind them.

Then, suddenly, a wall of frozen mist came down in front of them. Mark and Wolf could not get into the forest. Something was blocking them. When they had rescued the Swan Princess they had just gone straight to Swan Lake. Now they couldn't move. They were both soaking wet and they could hardly breathe.

"The Shape-changer," shouted Wolf.

"She's trapping us," whispered Mark. His throat was full of the terrible choking mist.

"Quick," said Wolf. "We must run. This mist might kill us."

"I can't," whispered Mark. "She's got me." The frozen mist was all around him now. Mark felt like a heavy log of wood. The mist seemed to be tying him up with ropes of steel.

"Hang on to me," shouted Wolf. "I'll get you through it. My magic is stronger than the Shape-changer's magic."

Mark hung on. He could feel Wolf dragging him.

"Call my name, Mark," roared Wolf.

Mark made one last superhuman effort. He sucked in a breath and shouted: "Wolf!"

The word echoed through the trees and came back to his ears.

For a moment things got better.

He was able to move his legs.

Now he was able to run beside Wolf. The mist was not so thick.

Then Wolf turned and everything seemed to get worse. The dry leaves of the forest were no longer under their feet. The ground was just slippery, wet rock. Mark felt himself falling. He stretched out his hand but there were no trees. There was nothing but rock walls all around them.

He heard squeaking noises in his ears.

Small winds blew around his face.

A claw touched his neck.

A small body bumped against his head.

Wolf stopped. Bit by bit, the mist cleared. Mark took a deep breath. He could hear the roar of a river beside them. They were in a cave. And they were not alone.

The cave was full of thousands of bats!

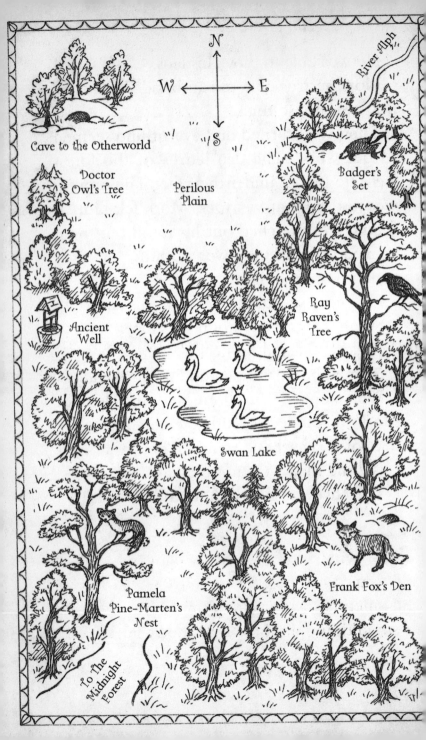

Chapter One

It was the last week of term before Christmas. Mark always liked the last week but this Monday he felt a bit fed-up. His mum had to go to Germany on business for five days. This meant that Nosy Nora, his horrible baby-sitter, would be around all the time.

"Horrible old Nosy Nora," Mark muttered to Wolf, his German shepherd puppy. Wolf was now four months old. He gave Mark a lick with his hot pink tongue. He hated Nosy Nora just as much as Mark did. Sometimes Mark didn't think that he could stand things at home if he didn't have Wolf.

Everything was also better in school since Mark had got Wolf. Raymond McCann and his friends had not bullied Mark as much. Raymond liked coming to Mark's house to play with Wolf. Miss Thompson, the teacher at school, had also helped. She had given Mark a few tips about standing up to Raymond.

"Act," said Miss Thompson. "You're a good actor. Act as if you're not afraid of him."

Mark had tried this. It seemed to work a bit.

"It might be that Raymond is a bit scared of Miss Thompson, though," Mark said to

6

Wolf. He was combing him on Monday before school. Wolf quite liked Raymond. This made Mark think that Raymond was not too bad. In a way, Raymond was now a sort of friend. At least he had stopped teasing Mark all the time.

But that Monday morning a new boy came to the class. His name was Sam Soper. He told everyone to call him Soapy. Soapy was very tough. He was so tough that even Raymond was a bit scared of him. Soapy's hair was very short and spiky. He was the biggest boy in the class. He wore an earring.

"Don't come to school wearing that earring again, Sam, please," said Miss Thompson.

"I've got to, Miss," said Soapy. "My Dad says I've got to."

"Well, I say you can't," said Miss Thompson. "It is against the school rules."

When she turned away, Soapy stuck out his tongue at her.

"You're a geek," he said to Mark at playtime.

Mark didn't say anything. He just turned away. It was no good, though.

"Don't you know it's polite to share?" asked Soapy. He grabbed Mark's bag of crisps and started to eat them.

"Give them back," said Mark. He tried to act tough. Soapy took no notice.

"Get the vinegar ones next time," he said. "I like them better than cheese and onion."

"Are you coming home with me today?" Mark asked Raymond. He thought Soapy might not bully him if he knew Raymond was his friend.

"Go home with a geek like you!" shouted Raymond. "What do you think I am? Get lost! We don't want you hanging around." Then he hit Mark. The slap made Mark feel like his head might drop off. Soapy laughed and Raymond's gang all cheered. Mark looked over at his friend James to see if he would help. James just walked away. He was leaving school the next day to go back to his old school. *I'd have stood up for him*, thought Mark bitterly. *I suppose he doesn't care because he's leaving.*

"And James didn't even say goodbye to me before he went," said Mark to Wolf after school. "And now, tomorrow, I won't have anyone sitting beside me." He hugged Wolf to cheer himself up.

The next day Soapy came to school without his earring. He wore a silver stud instead. Mark thought he looked just as tough. As he went past Mark's desk Soapy pushed all Mark's books onto the floor.

Wednesday and Thursday were just as bad. Mark could hardly wait for Friday to come.

On the last day of term Mark took his mobile phone to school. His mother had promised to ring him from the airport.

"If everything goes well on the trip, Mark," she'd said, before she left, "I'll be able to take next week off work. We'll give Nora a holiday and you and I will have fun getting everything ready for Christmas."

When 12.00 o'clock came, Mark grabbed his mobile and went outside.

"Mum's plane is due at 12.15," he muttered, munching his sandwiches, "but I'll switch my phone on now just in case she's early."

He was just about to put in his code number when a hand came down and grabbed it.

"Just what I wanted," said Soapy, "a nice, fancy mobile. Thank you giving it to me." He ran away across the playground.

"Give it back," yelled Mark, chasing him.

"Sorry," said Soapy, holding out the phone.

Mark's hand had just touched the phone when Soapy whipped it away.

Raymond and his friends were all laughing. Every time Mark got near the phone, Soapy ran faster. Then he would wait for Mark to catch up again. This went on for ages.

"It's no good to you, anyway," said Mark in the end. "You need to know the code to unlock it and I'm not telling you what it is."

"Torture him," said John.

"Nah," said Raymond McCann. Everyone looked at him in surprise. "Tommy will have a fit if you do," he said quickly. "Tommy" was Miss Thompson.

"I don't care anyway," said Soapy. "I don't need the code. That's dangerous. The police could get on to you. My dad will just whip out the SIM card and stick it into another case. New phone, no questions asked."

Mark looked at his watch. It was now nearly half past twelve. His mother would be trying to ring him. He was beginning to feel desperate.

"Give me my phone back, or else I am going to tell Miss Thompson," he said as bravely as he could.

"He won't dare," said John.

"Yes, I will," shouted Mark.

Before anyone could stop him, he dashed over and banged on the office door.

"Yes, Mark," said Miss Thompson smiling.

"Sam Soper has stolen my mobile and he won't give it back," explained Mark.

"That boy!" muttered Miss Thompson. She marched across the playground.

"Have you got Mark's phone, Sam?" she asked. Even Soapy looked a bit nervous at the sound of her voice. He held out the phone immediately.

"Yes, Miss," he said. "Here you are, Mark. It was just a joke, Miss. I was just fooling around."

"That's not the sort of thing that the police call a joke," said Miss Thompson. "The police call that stealing, and the courts put people

in jail for things like that. Think about that the next time you feel like playing a joke." She turned on her heel and then swung around again just in time to see Soapy sticking out his tongue.

Oh, and, Sam," she said. "We don't have any bullying at this school. If I see any bullying going on, I will send for your parents."

Mark sat outside the office window and switched on his phone. He kept staring at it, hoping that it would ring. It didn't. His mother was probably back at her office by now. He kept on acting as if he were listening to the phone. He was pretending that he didn't hear all the boys in the playground whispering: "Marky, Marky, teacher's pet."

"Your mother rang," said Nora when she met him after school. She grabbed his hand. "She has the week off next week. I'm going to have a holiday. And I can tell you I need it! That puppy of yours is driving me mad."

"Look at baby with his baby-sitter," sneered Raymond, from across the road.

"How's little Marky," shouted Soapy.

Mark didn't care. He pulled his hand out of Nora's grip and ran to his own gate.

Wolf was in the garden, waiting for Mark. His tail was wagging and he was yelping with excitement. Mark opened the pen and put his arms around Wolf's solid little body. He didn't care if he was getting muddy. It didn't matter. There would be no more school for nearly three weeks.

"No horrible old Nosy Nora, no Raymond, no Soapy, just you and me, little Mr Wolf," he said into Wolf's soft warm ear.

Chapter Two

It was going to be Wolf's first Christmas.
Mum had brought back a digital camera
from Germany. Mark's dad used it to take
some great photos of Wolf and Mark. There
was one that he really liked. Wolf had his
two ears standing up, carefully balanced
against each other.

"I'm going to make my Christmas cards
with that photo of you, Wolf," said Mark on
Saturday morning.

Wolf wagged his tail as Mark tickled him
under the chin. Mark plugged the camera
into his computer.

"Look, Wolf," he said as he opened up the
file. "I'm going to put a ring of holly as a

border. Then I'll put 'Happy Christmas from Mark & Wolf'." But Wolf wasn't listening to Mark. He was looking at the bedroom door and sniffing loudly.

"You're right, Wolf," said Mark stopping and sniffing the air. "The mince pies are beginning to burn Mum," he yelled.

"Mum!" he yelled again, but there was no sound from his mother in the kitchen.

"Let's find her, Wolf," he said.

"Mark," whispered Mum's voice from his parents' bedroom. It sounded as if she were crying or something. Mark opened the bedroom door. His mum was lying on the bed.

"Mark, get me my mobile from the study. I must phone the doctor. I've got the most terrible pain and I keep getting sick."

Mark quickly got the phone. Mum rang the doctor, but she still looked very sick. Mark had an idea. He got his own phone and rang his dad.

"Dad," he said, "Dad, come home quickly. Mum's very sick."

The doctor came and Dad rushed home from work. Then Wolf was locked in the kitchen while Mark and his dad took his mum to the hospital.

"It's her appendix," said Dad. "The doctor will take it out and she'll be back home again in time for Christmas. Don't worry!"

Mark nodded. He had a big lump in his throat.

"Come on, cheer up," said Dad. "Let's go home. We can get a 'take-away' on the way."

When they got home Mark couldn't eat anything. The lump in his throat was too big.

"Cheer up," said Dad again. "You and

Wolf can watch a video. Go and ask him what he wants to watch."

Mark tried to smile. He sat on the couch and buried his face in Wolf's soft fur. Wolf wouldn't mind if he cried. He would just lick the tears away with his hot tongue.

The next few days were horrible. Dad was too busy to take Mark to see his mum in hospital. His dad asked Nora to take Mark but she wouldn't go.

"Mum's fine, Mark," Dad kept saying. "She'll be home on Wednesday. You see I have this huge project on. I just can't spare a minute during the day and children aren't allowed into the hospital after five o'clock. She sent you her love."

Mark just nodded. He didn't want to be a nuisance. He did keep wondering, though, if everything was really all right. All last week when things had been bad at school, he had been looking forward to getting ready for Christmas. Now everything was ruined. His mother was in hospital. There would be no decorating the house and no Christmas tree. There probably wouldn't be many presents.

His father would be too busy. And of course, instead of having Mum to look after him this week, Nosy Nora had to come back. Poor Wolf had to stay outside in his pen instead of playing inside with Mark.

It was the worst time in Mark's life.

"Your dad won't be home until midnight," said Nora on Tuesday. "I have to stay the night. And I don't think your mum will be coming out of hospital tomorrow, either," she added. "Your dad said the hospital told him she had a bad night." Nora looked pleased when she said that.

That night when he went to bed Mark could not stop himself from crying. *There'll be no Christmas this year*, he thought.

Chapter Three

"Welcome, welcome to the Midnight Forest!"

Mark gave a jump. On the rock, just a few inches from his nose, was a tiny bat.

"This is Mark, Abraham," said Wolf.

Abraham gave a little bow, stretching out his five-fingered wings.

"Welcome, Mark," he said. "We heard your voice shouting 'Wolf' so we went to your rescue. The law of the Midnight Forest says that anyone who calls for help in the name of Wolf has to be answered. We brought you underground."

"I've never been down here before," said Wolf. "So this is Alph, the sacred river."

"Yes, the River Alph runs underground all the way around the forest," said Abraham. "Oh Wolf, there is terrible trouble in the forest! You and Mark must go there as fast as you can. The Shape-changer has put a wall of frozen mist around it. Nothing can get in or out until the wall of mist is lifted. We'll get you in by going underground."

"How will we find our way?" asked Wolf.

"We'll send two of the young ones to guide you," said Abraham. "Beeper and Cheeper are just the right age. In another

20

month or so their voices will be too high for humans to hear."

Beeper and Cheeper were a cheerful pair. They flew just in front of Mark and Wolf.

"Are you the ones that rescued the Swan Princess?" asked Beeper.

"Yes," said Mark. He felt rather proud.

"You're famous, you know," said Cheeper. "Me and Beeper made up a song about you."

Without waiting for Mark to say anything, they both began singing:

"Mark and Wolf are the best,
Cooler by far than all the rest,
So if you've got a job to do,
Just send Pam for the deadly two — "

"Where is Pamela?" interrupted Wolf.

"Gorgeous Pam," said Beeper. "She was too scared to come down here."

"What do you get if you put a bell tower with a bat?" asked Cheeper.

"Bats in the belfry," said Mark.

"Right," said Cheeper.

"What do you get if you put a man with a bat?" asked Beeper.

"That's easy. Batman," said Mark.

"Right," said Cheeper.

"Wrong," said Beeper. "You get AARAGH!" He screamed so loudly that even Wolf jumped. Mark had to laugh.

"What do you get if you put a man with a bat and they rob a bank?" asked Mark.

"No idea," said Beeper after a minute.

"Give up," said Cheeper.

"Batman and Robin," said Mark.

"Nice one," said Beeper.

Then they both fell about laughing so much that they almost fell into the River Alph.

"No fooling," said Wolf. "If you fall in there we might never get you out again."

"The passage twists and turns here," said Cheeper. "Keep listening for our pip-pips."

Mark listened carefully. The passageway was even darker now.

"Going uphill, now " said Beeper. "Get ready for a climb."

"What do you get if you put a bat with a hill?" asked Cheeper.

"A *bathill*? Oh, I know a battle," said Mark.

"You're pretty smart," said Beeper.

"No more talking," said Wolf. "We must be coming out soon. You never know, the Shape-changer might be around."

The two cheerful bats went very quiet. *The word Shape-changer is enough to frighten all the animals, except Wolf*, thought Mark.

They'd been walking for a good while when Mark finally saw some light. The underground passageway started to get brighter.

"No mist," whispered Mark to Wolf.

Wolf nodded. "We're well inside the forest, now," he whispered back. "The Shapechanger is trying to keep something from getting into the forest. I wonder what it is."

★ ★ ★ ★

"Hello, darlings," said Pamela Pine-Marten with her husky voice. She was a beautiful animal. She was about the size of a small dog. Her fur was a mixture of brown, red and gold. It shone in the light of the moon.

"Don't touch my hair, my loves," she said. "I can't bear bats in my hair!"

"We'll be off," said Cheeper.

"Bye, Mark," said Beeper. They went swooping back down the passageway. As they went, Mark could hear Beeper say: "What do you get if you put a bat with a crow?"

"Hallo, Pamela," said Mark. He felt a bit shy of Pamela Pine-Marten. She was always telling him how handsome and brave he was. "You've got trouble, I hear," he added, trying to sound tough.

"Come and see for yourself," said Pamela. "Doctor Owl said to bring you to him."

The forest seems different tonight, thought Mark. He kept a tight grip on Wolf's shoulder. The Perilous Plain had disappeared. In its place there were some spiky, evil-looking pine trees.

"You go first, Wolf," said Pamela Pine-Marten. "Those pine branches will tear my fur and I've been to the hairdresser this morning."

"I'll hold the branches back for you, Pamela," said Mark.

"Come on," growled Wolf. "We've no time to waste. This is strong magic. The air stinks of it."

There was a strange smell in the air. It was a strong, sweet, disgusting smell. Mark knew what it meant. The Shape-changer was nearby. He did not allow himself to feel frightened, though. Once he was in the Midnight Forest and with Wolf, Mark felt as brave as a. . . . well, as brave as a wolf.

"So there you are," said Frank Fox suddenly popping out from behind a hedge. "We've been waiting for you."

"You've got a family since I saw you last," said Mark, looking at the foxes behind Frank.

"Yes," said Frank Fox proudly. "That's Freda, my wife, and Fred and Francie, my cubs."

"What's the problem, Frank?" asked Wolf.

"*She*'s stopped Christmas from coming to the Midnight Forest," said Frank Fox. "The children are so upset."

"Stopped Christmas!" shouted Wolf.

"Stopped Christmas," whispered Mark. He felt sick. This seemed like the most evil thing the Shape-changer had ever done.

"I want to have Christmas," wept Francie. Fred was sniffing hard, too. Mark stared at them feeling miserable.

Then, suddenly, there was a big shout nearby.

"We can get through!" the voice yelled. "The frozen mist is lifting."

"That's Benjy Badger," roared Wolf. "Quick, Mark. You know what that badger cub is like. He has no sense."

Mark dashed through the last few pine branches. They scratched him, but he didn't care. In front he had a confused feeling of seeing Christmas trees, and presents and decorations. But then, a moment later, there was only a solid wall of frozen mist. Bert Badger had grabbed Benjy.

"Oh, Dad," shouted Benjy. "I could have got into the Christmas place."

"You stay where you are, my lad, or you'll get a clip around the ear," threatened Bert. "You don't know what might happen to you if you go in there. That's not Christmas. There's black magic in there."

"It's Wolf and Mark!" shouted Buster, Benjy's brother.

"You're very welcome, both of you," said Bert. "You can see the trouble we have."

"That Shape-changer is wicked, through and through," said Mrs Badger crossly. "She keeps letting the children have a glimpse of Christmas just to tease them. Then she brings down the wall of frozen mist again."

"It's not just to tease them, Bridie," said Doctor Owl, flying down. "This is one of the Shape-changer's evil plans."

"She's trying to get hold of the children, is she?" asked Wolf.

Bridie Badger gripped Buster and Barbie tightly and Bert grabbed Benjy's paw. Mark saw that under the pines there were more children. Rosie Squirrel was there with four baby squirrels. Even Doctor Owl had a small model of himself. The young owl was sitting silently on a low branch.

"Look!" everyone shouted.

Suddenly the wall of frozen mist seemed to part in the middle. It looked like the curtain in a theatre. The smell of the Shape-changer got very strong. Then all of a sudden it disappeared. Everyone started to sniff. What was that smell?

There was a smell of hot mince pies.

There was a smell of roast turkey.

There was a spicy smell of Christmas trees.

And then the music began. It was *Jingle Bells*. The air was full of the sound of Mark's favourite Christmas carol. Then, worst of all, the children heard the sound of Christmas wrapping paper being torn open.

Four little rabbits ran forward and the baby squirrels shot down from the tree, the small owl fluttered his wings. Benjy twisted himself loose, and then. . . .

Chapter Four

Wolf shot forward. The wall of frozen mist was gone but now Wolf blocked the way. He ran up and down. He barked and growled. He even gave Benjy a small nip. He ran so fast, and he twisted and turned so cleverly, that none of the small animals could get past him. He was like a living, moving wall. He stopped all the small animals from going forward.

"I'll help you, Wolf," shouted Mark. He grabbed two small rabbits. Quickly he handed them over to their mother. He picked up the little squirrels and gave them to Rosie.

Then Mark heard something strange. He looked around. He could still hear *Jingle Bells* but now somebody was singing. It sounded like his mum's voice. Somehow the singing made him feel more Christmassy than everything else.

"Mark, quick," shouted Wolf. Mark shook himself. He had to help Wolf. Benjy had managed to escape again. He was dashing forward.

"Benjy," screamed Bridie.

Mark took a flying leap after Benjy. It was a great jump, just like Raymond McCann would do on the football field. For a moment he felt a wet, sweet-smelling mist all over his face. Then, next moment, he had rolled over backwards, still holding Benjy. Wolf's shoulder was at his head.

"All right, Mark?" asked Wolf.

"Fine," said Mark, getting up. He gave Benjy back to Bert. Then he went on grabbing more small animals. All the time, though, he was hearing his mother singing.

"The mist is coming back," shouted Buster Badger.

"You're right," said Bridie. "Let's get all the children home before anything bad happens."

"Good idea," said Frank Fox. "To be perfectly frank and honest with you. . . ."

"Oh, come on," growled Doctor Owl. "Cut the talking and get the kids home."

"You and I will go at the back, Mark," said Wolf. "We'll make sure nobody gets lost."

So all the animals of the Midnight Forest set off walking or flying through the spiky pines carrying or dragging their children. When they reached the edge of the Perilous Plain, Pamela Pine-Marten went one way. The foxes went the other way, and the squirrels rushed up an ash tree. The owls flew to their tree. Wolf and Mark followed the badgers.

They were almost there when Mark felt his legs get heavier, and heavier. He took his hand off Wolf's shoulder. He just could not make himself walk as fast as Wolf.

"Mark," came a whisper.

Who was it? Mark turned his head. There was no one there. Was it Pamela Pine-Marten?

"Mark," came the whisper again. Mark stopped. Wolf stopped as well.

"Come on, Mark," he said.

"Just tying my shoelace," said Mark. It was a lie. He untied the shoelace and then tied it up again. Wolf was still waiting. Now Mark was quite sure. It was definitely his mum's voice. She was singing *Jingle Bells* again.

"You go on, Wolf," he said. "I'll catch up."

"No . . ." began Wolf, but at that very moment a baby rabbit shot back shouting,

"Chwistmas! Me want Chwistmas!" Wolf caught it and started back towards Mrs Rabbit. Mark turned and bolted towards the sound of the singing voice. He wanted to find it.

Suddenly it was really easy to go through those spiky pine trees. The branches seemed to let him go through. Mark began to run.

"Mark," came the whisper again. The voice was getting louder now. There was a sharp smell. It wasn't the sweet disgusting Shape-changer's smell. This was a different smell. Of course! It was the smell of a hospital. Mum must be near. Mark stopped. Suddenly his legs began to shake.

"He's afraid," said a voice.

"Baby," said another voice. The voices came from the trees above him. One was Ray Raven.

"He's a cry-baby, he's a cry-baby, he's a cry-baby," chanted Ray Raven. "Look at him, Soapy, he's going to cry."

Soapy was a stoat. Mark could see an evil, savage mouth with large teeth. Soapy had a short blunt head with spiky fur sticking up from his low forehead. Mark felt very afraid of him. He hated stoats.

"Come on, Marky," said Soapy Stoat. "Mummy wants to see you. She's in there."

It was very misty now. Straight ahead of him Mark could just see a big tree. It was a very old tree. The trunk of the tree was huge. Halfway up the tree trunk was a large hole. Mark stared at the hole. There was no doubt about it. His mum's voice was coming out of that hole.

"Mark," she called. Her voice sounded faint and far away.

The mist filled Mark's eyes. He blinked. The hole in the tree seemed to be a window now. Through that window he could see a hospital ward. His mum was lying on a bed. Her arms were held out as if she was calling him.

"Mum!" he shouted.

Then a door seemed to open in the tree trunk. It was definitely the hospital. Mark could see doctors and nurses in a long corridor.

"Mark!" This was not Mum's voice. It was another voice. It was deeper and rougher. It was so rough that it broke up the picture of the hospital. The tree became a hollow tree trunk again.

"Wolf," cried Mark. He had left Wolf without any help. He had to go back. Mark tried to pull himself away from the tree. It felt as if he were tied to it by a giant rubber band.

"Get away, you rotten old Shape-changer," he screamed. "Leave me alone. You're just trying to trick me."

Suddenly Mark's face felt drier. The mist was not so thick now.

"Wolf, help me!" he shouted.

Wolf came crashing through the pine trees snarling loudly. Ray Raven shot off. He made a caw-caw noise but he sounded a bit afraid. Soapy Stoat turned and vanished in a second. The frozen mist seemed to melt away and so did the smell of the hospital.

"Oh, Wolf," said Mark putting his two arms around Wolf's neck. "Mum is calling me. What's wrong? Is she very sick?"

Chapter Five

"It was just black magic," said Bert Badger.

Mark looked around the badgers' kitchen and took a deep breath. It was lovely to be there again. He was sitting in front of a blazing wood fire, glancing around. *It's the nicest room in the world*, thought Mark.

"It wasn't your mum, love," said Bridie Badger. "It was just the Shape-changer whispering."

"I'm not afraid of the Shape-changer," said Benjy, but he was looking nervously into the dark corner, where Bert Badger kept his bottles of homemade wine.

Mark laughed. He was feeling better now. Wolf and Bert had explained everything to him. It wasn't his mother calling him. It was just one of the Shape-changer's tricks. He warmed his cold hands on the hot mug of elderberry wine.

"Nothing like a good fire to get the taste of the mist out of your mouth," said Bert. "Now what can we do, Wolf? We're relying on you and Mark to sort this out. If you can't help, there'll be no Christmas."

Wolf nodded. He looked very serious. "I think our only chance is that the Shape-changer seems frightened of me now. She runs away when I come near."

"But you can't be here all the time," said Bridie. "You and Mark have your own lives to lead. What are we going to do about Christmas?"

"I think we need Doctor Owl's help," said Wolf. "The more brains we can get working on this, the better."

"I'll go and get him," said Mark, draining the last of his elderberry wine. "Would you like to come with me, Barbie?" He didn't feel like trying to control Benjy, but Barbie was a sweet little thing.

"Will you be all right?" asked Bridie.

"They'll be fine," said Wolf. "The Shape-changer has had a fright. She'll try something different now. Mark stood up to her that time, so she'll leave him alone for a while."

Barbie put on her pink hat and her pink scarf and then put her paw in Mark's hand. He felt very grown-up as Wolf walked them to the door.

"Oh, look, it's beginning to snow," said Barbie, as they hurried along. She began to jump up and down. "It's going to be snowing for Christmas," she sang the words just like a little song. "You and Wolf are going to make sure that we have Christmas, aren't you, Mark? Promise!"

"I promise," said Mark. He hoped he would be able to keep his promise. The forest still did not look right, he thought. He said nothing to Barbie, though. He did not want to worry her.

A shower of loose snow suddenly fell from the branch above them. Mark looked up. It was Ray Raven. Mark took a deep breath. He had to be brave, now.

"I wanted to see you, Ray Raven," he said. "Wolf has sent me to find Doctor Owl. Take us the right way, will you?"

That was just the way his dad talked. Mark thought it might work with Ray Raven.

Ray Raven seemed to think for a moment. "OK, follow me," he said.

It worked! thought Mark.

Barbie could not walk very fast, but Ray Raven did not rush them. He flew just ahead until they came to Doctor Owl's tree.

"Thank you," said Mark cheerfully.

"Geek!" said Ray Raven. He flew away cawing scornfully.

Mark shrugged his shoulders. At least Ray Raven had taken them the right way.

"I don't like him much, anyway," Mark said to Barbie. "I'm not going to bother trying to be friends with him, anymore." He reached up and knocked with a stick on Doctor Owl's door.

"Yes," said Doctor Owl, looking down.

"Wolf would like to see you, Doctor Owl. He's over in Bert's place. He said he needed all the brains he could find," he added.

Doctor Owl looked pleased. "I'll just fly over there, then," he said. "You and Barbie follow me. You won't get lost if you go straight home. It's only if you go away from home that you get lost."

With that Doctor Owl flew off silently.

"Come on, Barbie," said Mark.

Doctor Owl was right. It seemed to be easy to find the way back. Mark could recognise everything now.

"Oh, look," said Barbie. "There's Francie and Fred Fox. Where are they going?"

The two small foxes were creeping along the edge of the Perilous Plain.

"Let's follow them," said Mark in a low voice. "I don't think their mum and dad know that they are out. They keep looking over their shoulders."

"And there's Becky and Rascal Rabbit," said Barbie. "There must be something exciting going to happen."

It might be the Shape-changer again, thought Mark. He felt suddenly cold and frightened.

"Oh look!" said Barbie again. "It's a Christmas shop!"

There was a long table set-up with a red and white striped cloth. On the table there were lots of toys. Someone was standing behind the table. It was Soapy Stoat.

"Come on, kids," he shouted. "Look at these toys. Best value in town. Everything is half price. Now, Mr Fox, what about a car for you? Have a good look at it. Go on, touch it."

Fred Fox touched the car. *It's cheap rubbish*, thought Mark. "Those wheels will fall off as soon as you play with it, Fred," he said aloud.

"You buzz off or you'll get bitten," whispered Soapy Stoat to Mark. He showed his sharp teeth in an evil smile.

"Your Dad will be cross, Fred," shouted Mark. "You'd better get home all of you."

"Hello, darlings,' said a voice from behind. "Oh, a shop!" It was Pamela Pine-Marten. "Don't touch my fur, darlings," she added to the little rabbits. She went up to the back of the stall saying, "Stay with Mark, darlings. He'll look after you."

"Have you got anything for little me in your shop?" she asked, smiling sweetly at Soapy Stoat.

"I have only one thing good enough for a beautiful lady like you," said Soapy Stoat. He took out a small glass bottle.

"This perfume comes from Paris," he said. "You'd die of shock if I told you the price, but I'll tell you what I'll do. It's not often I see a lady as beautiful as you so I'll give it to you at half price.

"Let me smell it," said Pamela. She looked very pleased at being called beautiful.

Soapy Stoat opened the glass bottle and held it out. Mark stepped forward. Inside the bottle there was a thick green liquid. It was a sweet, sickly disgusting smell. It smelt of the Shape-changer.

"Don't touch it, Pamela," he shouted. "There's black magic in that. You'll be in the Shape-changer's power if you touch that."

Soapy Stoat's grin vanished. Suddenly he looked so dangerous that Mark took a quick step backwards. *Why did I come out without Wolf,* he thought. *Soapy Stoat looks as if he could kill me.*

"Scared?" whispered Soapy in Mark's ear. Then with the oily grin back on his face again he turned back to Pamela.

"Try some on your fur," he said. "Mark is just a kid. He doesn't know what all the ladies in Paris are wearing this season."

Pamela stretched out her hand for the perfume, but suddenly Mark's courage came back. He grabbed the bottle and threw it as far away as he could. It flew over the trees. There was a sudden terrible smell. Then the sky cleared and Mark knew what he should do.

"Come on, everyone," he shouted. "It's a race. The first person home will have the best Christmas present in the world."

He watched as all the small animals ran as fast as they could go. He had no worries about them now.

"Let's get home, Barbie," said Mark. "Your Mum will be wondering where you are."

Chapter Six

"So there you are," said Bert Badger. "We've been waiting for you. We've run out of ideas."

Mark felt a bit embarrassed. He sat down in front of the fire. He couldn't think of anything to say.

"All right, Mark?" asked Wolf, putting a heavy paw on Mark's knee.

"Fine," said Mark.

"A stoat was selling Christmas toys," said Barbie chattily. "He was trying to make all of us buy them, but Mark wouldn't let us. Then he tried to sell perfume to Pamela Pine-Marten and Mark took the bottle and he *frowed* it away over the trees."

"Soapy Stoat?" asked Doctor Owl.

Mark nodded. "I bet that he's one of the Shape-changer's men. I smelt her horrible smell from the perfume," he said calmly. "I dealt with him."

"I knew you could," said Wolf.

"Is it still misty out there?" asked Benjy.

"Yes," said Mark.

"I hate mist in the winter," said Bridie. "It doesn't matter in the summer. The sun burns it off, but in the winter it hangs around."

Mark nodded again. He was beginning to feel sleepy. He half closed his eyes, but then he opened them again.

"Burn it off," he said slowly. Everyone turned around to stare at him. He jumped to his feet. He didn't feel a bit sleepy now.

"That's the second time that you've said something like that," he said to Bridie. He felt so excited that the words were just tumbling out of him. "Earlier you, or was it Bert, said: 'Nothing like a good fire to get the taste of mist out of your mouth.' Has anyone here ever seen the Shape-changer in a house by the fire?'"

"Never," said Bert, staring at Mark.

"No one has ever seen her properly. No one knows what she really looks like. She keeps changing shape," added Bridie. 'But you're right. She's only ever seen out in the forest.'

"But we can't stay indoors for our whole lives just to escape her," said Doctor Owl.

"Let Mark explain," said Wolf.

"We can make a fire outside," said Mark. "We can get everyone in the forest to help. We can light a huge fire under the wall of frozen mist. It will burn the frozen mist and the Shape-changer will disappear."

"You're the lad with brains," said Bert as Benjy, Buster and Barbie all clapped.

"We'll need to tell everyone in the whole forest," said Doctor Owl.

"There's only one way to do that," said Bert Badger.

They both stared at each other. Their faces were very serious.

"It's time for the Great Bell," said Bert.

"The Great Bell," whispered Buster to Benjy.

"The Great Bell," echoed Bridie.

Bert went to a shelf high in the wall. He was muttering to himself: "Now where did I put that key. I wish people would stop tidying up after me."

"It's in your tool box," said Bridie calmly.

Bert dug deep into his tool box. He was scattering tools all over the floor. He finally held up a key, the size of his paw.

"The Great Bell is in the cellar," he said.

Mark and Wolf followed him down the steps. Doctor Owl fluttered on ahead.

The cellar was huge. In its centre there was an enormous central heating boiler chugging away.

"Now where is it?" muttered Bert.

"Third box on the left hand wall near the door," called down Bridie.

Bert gave a grunt of satisfaction. He opened the third box. Slowly and carefully he lifted out the Great Bell.

"This is the Great Bell of the Midnight Forest," he said. He held it up for them to see.

The Great Bell was made from bronze. It had strange markings on it. *They're just like the markings on that ancient stone we found when we rescued the Swan Princess* thought Mark.

Bert Badger gave the Great Bell to Wolf. "The law of the Midnight Forest says that Wolf rings the Great Bell, "said Bert.

Mark felt very proud to be Wolf's best friend. He walked behind him as Wolf climbed the stairs. They went down the passageway and out the door. All the badgers followed. Mark stood beside Bert as Wolf swung the Great Bell up and down. It filled the forest with a hollow booming noise.

For a few minutes nothing happened. Then Wolf swung the Great Bell again and again. Suddenly the air was full of sound. Mark could hear doors slamming, wings beating, and small feet scurrying. In a moment all the hares, rabbits, field mice, owls, the Royal Swans, the moles, the shrews, the foxes and the bats were there. Last of all, of course, Pamela Pine-Marten, arrived.

"Friends," said Wolf. "Mark has found the answer to the Shape-changer's evil magic. We can fight her and we will win. We must light a big fire to burn the frozen mist. If we do this then the children can have their Christmas."

There was a great cheer. All the animals started jumping up and down. The birds and bats flew round and round in circles. They made a huge noise. Mark felt himself getting very red. Even Pamela Pine-Marten was clapping her elegant paws together so she wasn't cross with him for throwing the perfume away.

"Wait a minute," said Bert Badger. "We must plan this. We'll all go through the forest until we reach the wall of frozen mist. Everyone must pick up as many branches and twigs as they can manage. The small animals can bring fir cones. Buster, go get my lantern from the kitchen. Bring in out carefully."

"I'll carry the lantern," said Pamela Pine-Marten. "I wouldn't be too good at carrying branches. I have to look after my fur and my nails, you know."

So Pamela led the way. Wolf and Mark were just behind her. Wolf showed Mark how to wind long strings of ivy around the branches to make a big bundle. Even the

tiniest field-mice children were rolling fir cones
along. The Royal Swans flew above the trees
snapping off branches with their beaks.

By the time that they reached the wall of
frozen mist they had heaps and heaps of
wood. Bert, Mark and Wolf went up and
down the line, piling everything up. They
made sure that there were plenty of fir cones
under each pile. The cones would give the
fire a good start.

"Stand back, everyone," roared Wolf. "Bert, start the fire."

So Bert Badger took a newly broken piece of pine and pushed it into the flame of his lantern. It blazed up. Then he touched a pile of fir cones with the stick and they blazed up. He touched another pile and another, until the whole line was blazing away.

Suddenly, there was a scream. From behind the wall of melting mist a strange swirling shape rose up. It seemed to break through the branches of the trees and disappear into the midnight sky.

Most of the animals ran away when they heard the terrible scream. The birds and bats flew high up on to the trees. Mark shut his eyes and stuck his fingers in his ears. He didn't want to hear the words in that scream. They were not bad words. The words seemed to be in a different language, but they were very scary. Mark moved so that his leg was touching Wolf's shoulder. He gripped Wolf's warm fur. Then the noise died down and finally it stopped.

Chapter Seven

Mark opened his eyes. The first thing he noticed was that the frozen mist was gone. The air seemed dryer. Everybody was standing very still. The moon and the stars were shining silver in the midnight sky. It started snowing.

The moonlight shone along a path of pine trees. Red, yellow and blue lanterns hung from every tree. There were little shops all along the pathway. They were crammed with presents and Christmas decorations.

"Oh, look," said Barbie. "It's Christmas."

"All the shops are open," shouted Buster.

Suddenly everyone started to run. Some of the animals ran behind the counters of the little shops and started selling.

"Oh, look, Wolf!" said Mark. Right in front of them was a shop piled high with shining red and gold foil-wrapped present and Christmas stockings and dark green holly branches.

"Rosie Red Squirrel is roasting chestnuts," shouted Buster.

"Let's get some, Wolf," said Mark.

"Oh Barbie," screamed Francie Fox. "Look at the little red feather scarves that Robin is selling. Oh, I'd love one of those."

"I'll buy you one," said Mark. He took out his pocket money and paid Robin.

"Would you like one, Barbie?" He asked, but Barbie shook her head.

"I'd like some furniture for my dolls' house," she said. "Look at the field mice's stall over there." The field mice were selling dolls' furniture made from acorn and hazelnut shells. Mark bought her a little cupboard and two baby-dolls' cradles.

"What would you like, Fred?" he asked. He felt pleased that he always had so much pocket money. It was great fun buying presents. Fred was a shy little fox, much shyer than his sister, Francie.

Eventually he whispered into Mark's ear: "I'd like a skipping rope from Mr Hedgehog."

Mr Hedgehog had a great selection. "I'd advise ivy, myself, if you are going in for some good hard training, " he said to Fred. "Honeysuckles make a good rope too, but they break if you use them too much."

So Mark bought a skipping rope made from ivy for Fred. He got a silver brooch from a magpie for the Swan Princess and a wooden whistle that made a rude noise for Benjy. He even got a smart bow tie for Buster.

On another stall, Mr Mole, in his velvet suit, was selling some potted plants and gardening stuff. Mark bought a Christmas rose for Mrs Badger and a good-sized shovel for Bert.

Beeper and Cheeper were selling joke books on one stall.

"Hi, Mark," they shouted. "What do you get if you put a crow with a bat?"

"Can't guess," shouted Mark.

"Acrobat," yelled Beeper. "Get it? A-crow-bat. Acrobat!"

Mark laughed and waved to them. There were lots of small animals gathered around their stall, giggling at the jokes.

Wolf and Mark wandered around the Christmas Fair watching everyone enjoying the fun. Bridie Badger was buying apple pies from a fat hen pheasant and Pamela Pine-Marten was buying a new hairbrush from Mrs Hedgehog.

At the far end of the Christmas Fair, Harry Hare was selling Christmas trees decorated with silver spiderwebs and red holly berries.

"I'll give you a hand with these trees, mate," said Soapy Stoat, suddenly appearing from behind Harry Hare.

"Buzz off," shouted Mark. "We don't want any of your sort around here." He couldn't believe that he had the courage to say that. The words seemed to go straight from his brain to his mouth. They just came out.

Harry Hare was astonished. He looked from Mark to Soapy Stoat with his mouth open.

"It's your business of course, Harry," said Mark, "but I wouldn't trust that sort as far as

I would throw him. There, he's gone now. Someone was telling me that he's gone over to the Shape-changer's side. I bet he had a lorry tucked away somewhere and you'd lose half your trees if you turned your back on him," he added.

"Thanks, lad," said Harry Hare. "I'll keep a sharp lookout for Soapy Stoat in the future."

"Perhaps I shouldn't have said that," said Mark to Wolf, as they were walking over to Bert Badger's stall. Bert was now busily selling his homemade wines.

"You did the right thing," said Wolf. "Always stand up to those sort of people. They just take advantage of you if you are nice to them."

I must remember that, thought Mark. *I try to be friends with these bullies and I try to get them to like me. I'll just tell them to get lost in future.* He looked all around the Christmas Fair. He had plenty of good friends here, in the Midnight Forest, he thought.

"Time to go home, Mark," said Wolf. "There's going to be a good Christmas in the Midnight Forest after all!"

Chapter Eight

That must be a toy telephone, thought Mark sleepily, but then he woke up properly. It was his mobile ringing. The clock said 9:05! Mark jumped out of bed. Had he overslept, but no, of course, it was the holidays.

"Hello," he said answering his phone.

"Hiya!" It was Raymond McCann. Mark made a face.

"Are you there?" said Raymond. "I've nothing to do. I'll come around and play one of your computer games."

Suddenly Mark woke up completely. Why should Raymond McCann come around and play with his computer after hitting him like that in school? Anyway, the last time he messed up all the settings. *It took me ages to get it right again,* Mark remembered. *What was it Dad used to say when that man he didn't like kept asking him to play a game of golf?*

"No," he said, the words coming out before he had time to think about them. "Sorry, I'm too busy today."

There was a silence. Then came Raymond's voice, sounding very surprised. "OK," he said. "See you."

"See you," said Mark. He hung up before Raymond had a chance to say anything else.

"Yes!" he said, and punched the air. He had done it! He was not going to let Raymond McCann push him around anymore. He quickly had a shower. Then he dressed in his favourite jeans and sweatshirt and ran downstairs. He still had a big smile on his face.

"Up at last," snapped Nora, crashing dishes into the dishwasher. "When I was your age I couldn't stay in bed all the morning. Spoilt, that's what you are, if you ask me."

"No one's asking you," muttered Mark under his breath, but he took good care that she didn't hear him.

"Where's Wolf?" he asked aloud.

"Your Dad took him for a run. He put him in his pen when I arrived," snapped Nora. "I told him straight. I'm not having that animal in my nice clean kitchen. He said you were to feed him when you got up."

Mark went to the window and looked out. Wolf was standing up on his back legs in the pen and looking hopefully towards the kitchen.

"Where's Dad?" asked Mark.

"Gone to the hospital," said Nora. "He's gone to see your Mum. She might be able to come home today after all. The hospital said that she had a good night, your dad said to tell you," she added sourly.

"Great!" Mark's eyes shone. "I'll just go out and give Wolf his breakfast," he added.

"No, you won't," said Nora crossly. "You'll have your own breakfast first. That dog can wait."

Mark went half way to the table, but then he stopped. Wolf looked lonely and he was probably hungry, too.

"I always feed Wolf first. My Dad says that I must," he added. That was what Soapy always said.

It worked with Nora. She gave a sniff, but said no more. Mark carefully weighed out the right amount of dog biscuits.

Wolf was delighted to see Mark. The weather was cold. Mark's hands were freezing, but Wolf felt as warm as toast. They had a good run around the garden. Then Mark fed Wolf. He felt very happy. His mum would be home soon and they would have a lovely Christmas. Mark spread new straw in Wolf's kennel and put clean water in his drinking bucket. Then he went back inside to eat breakfast.

Mark had just finished when the mobile rang. He took a deep breath. It would be Raymond McCann again, he thought. Suddenly, with Nora's eye on him, he didn't feel so brave.

"Well, go on," said Nora crossly. "Answer it. A lot of nonsense, if you ask me! A phone of your own at eight years old! No wonder you're spoilt!"

"Hello!" said Mark in a whisper.

"Mark?" It was his dad. "Mark," he said again. "Can you hear me?"

"Yes, Dad," said Mark joyfully.

"Mark, I'll be bringing Mum home in an hour's time. She's fine. Tell Nora, will you? Make sure that everything is ready."

"Great," said Mark. He hung up and locked the phone. "Mum's coming home in an hour," he said. "Dad says you're to make sure that everything is ready for her."

Nora gave a sniff, but said nothing. She was a bit afraid of his father, Mark noticed. He must remember that. Perhaps he should take Miss Thompson's advice and act. He could act as if he were his father.

Could I do that? He wondered. Would it work?

He put his plate in the dishwasher. Then he went out into the garden without asking Nora if he could. He was going to stop letting her bully him, Mark decided. He would be polite, but if she tried to stop him doing things that his mum and dad always

allowed him to do he would take no notice of her.

"Let's find some flowers for Mum," he said to Wolf. At first there didn't seem to be anything, but then Wolf found one pure white, Christmas rose under a bush. Mark picked some pieces of holly to go with it. He ran inside and took a small vase from a kitchen cupboard. Nora had her mouth open to ask him what he was doing, but he flew upstairs. He put the vase on the table beside his mother's bed.

After that the time went very quickly. Mark had Wolf safely in his pen by the time, Mum got out of the car. She was looking pale. Dad and Mark quickly got her upstairs and into bed.

"What a lovely little vase of flowers!" was the first thing she said. Mark felt really pleased. And then, "Oh dear, however am I going to manage about Christmas?"

"Dad and I will do everything," said Mark.

"I've got the rest of the week off work, I've finished off that project," said Dad. "There'll be no problem. You'll see. It'll be the best Christmas we've ever had."

That very afternoon Dad, Mark and Wolf went out to the woods. They found enough holly and ivy to decorate a palace. Then they made a long list of everything they would need over Christmas, including some special treats for Wolf. Mark typed the list on to the supermarket's website. It was such a long list that when the van arrived it took nearly half an hour to unpack everything. And Nora didn't complain once! Not even when Dad laughed at the muddy pawmarks Wolf made all over the kitchen floor, when they came back from the woods.

Then, on Christmas Eve, it snowed, and it snowed. It was still snowing when Mark went to bed. As a special treat, Mark's mother said that Wolf could sleep in his bedroom for Christmas Eve. Wolf really loved snuggling down on his beanbag beside Mark's bed. It was much better than sleeping in the kitchen!

Chapter Nine

On Christmas morning Mark jumped out of bed and ran across to the window. "Yes!" he said. "Look, Wolf. There's been more snow during the night." He was so excited that he took Wolf out before he even looked at his Christmas stocking.

Wolf and Mark ran around the garden scattering snow everywhere. The snow was almost up to Wolf's chin, but he was a great jumper.

'You look like a husky dog, now, Wolf,' said Mark.

They went back into the kitchen to dry off. Then they went upstairs to open Mark's stocking.

"Guess what this is, Wolf," said Mark. He held out something long and hard for Wolf to sniff. It was a little telescope with a map of the stars wrapped around it. Mark was thrilled. The next present was a compass. There was a message written on the box: "For Finding Your Way through the Deepest Forest." Then Wolf's nose found something small. It was a whistle that only a dog could hear. Mark blew it and Wolf wagged his tail. Then there was a set of colouring pens and a pocket-sized computer game.

"Great," said Mark.

Before dinner was the main present-giving. Mum was able to get up for it and hand out the presents. Wolf got a beautiful new collar and lead. Mark got loads of stuff. He got some computer games for his PC, a new scarf and gloves and a book about badgers. Then only the biggest present of all was left. It was the size of a small cupboard. It looked as if it had taken a whole roll of red foil paper to wrap it up. Mark kept wondering if it was for him, and what it might be.

"To Mark and Wolf, from Mum and Dad," said Mum, reading out the card. She smiled at Mark who was so excited he couldn't speak. His Dad carried the present over. It only took Wolf and Mark a few seconds to rip off the paper. Then Wolf gave a big deep bark of excitement.

There on the floor was a magnificent sledge. It was made from polished wood. It had runners on either side, a seat at the back, and a rope on the front. Mark had never had such a good present before.

"Do you like it?" asked Mum.

"It's cool!" said Mark. His Mum and Dad were smiling. They could see how much he loved the sledge. He rushed over and gave his mum a big hug.

"We wanted to give you something special," said Mum. "You've been so good and helpful while I was sick."

"Can we take it to the park?" Mark asked, his voice trembling with excitement.

"After dinner," said his Dad. "Nora is just ready to dish up now. My word, Nora, what would we do without you? That smells great."

"Everything smells gorgeous Nora, thank you," said Mum. "Isn't Nora a wonderful cook, Mark?" she added.

Mark nodded but he didn't say anything. The food did look great, though. There was roast turkey, stuffing, ham, bread sauce, gravy, bacon rolls and all kinds of vegetables.

Before they started they pulled their crackers and even Dad put on a paper hat. Wolf barked at the bang. Mark put a purple hat over Wolf's two wobbly ears.

Mark felt so hungry that his tummy hurt. He liked everything on the table except the Brussel sprouts. He hated sprouts. He watched anxiously as Nora came around the table with the dish. Perhaps when she left he could ask Mum if he could leave them on the plate. The trouble was that he knew the smell of them, and the look of them, would spoil the rest of his dinner. What would his Dad do? Mark didn't know. Then, just as Nora's spoon, full of sprouts, was touching his plate, words popped out of his mouth.

"No, thank you, Nora, I never eat sprouts at Christmas." It was just the sort of thing his

Dad would say, he thought. Perhaps it would work.

Nora opened her mouth, but luckily Mark's Dad found this so funny that he laughed and laughed. His Dad laughed so much that Wolf came out from under the table. Nora gave a sour smile and took the sprouts away.

"I'll have my own dinner then," she said stiffly. "The trifle and the plates are on the sideboard."

As soon as the door closed behind her, Mark really enjoyed his dinner, but the best bit of all came about an hour after dinner. His Dad, who had been snoozing by the fire, suddenly woke-up and said: "Let's take the sledge of yours to the park, Mark."

"What about Mum?" asked Mark.

"I'll have a nice rest in bed," said Mum. "Nora will be here for another hour so. I'll get up for tea and we'll have the Christmas cake."

That was all right then. Mark put on his new scarf and gloves; Wolf had his new collar and lead. Then off they went, dragging the new sledge to the park.

The park was great fun. It had a small hill with some trees on the top of it. Mark pulled his sledge to the top and then shot back down.

"You and I will take turns at pulling the sledge up the hill," said Dad. "I need to work off my Christmas dinner."

Mark shot down the hill at least forty times, one after the other. Wolf galloping alongside him, barking joyfully.

"Just one more run down the hill," said Dad. "We'd better get back. I don't want your Mum to be alone."

So for a last time, Mark and Wolf flew down the hill. The sledge and Wolf's paws were scattering snow everywhere. As they went Wolf was barking and Mark was singing *Jingle Bells*.

It was Wolf's first Christmas and Mark's best Christmas ever.